THE WIND IN THE WILLOWS
Story Book

Abridged from
Kenneth Grahame's classic book

Illustrated by Ernest H. Shepard

DEAN

The Wind in the Willows originally published
8th October 1908 by Methuen & Co Ltd
This edition first published 1992
Reissued 1993 by Dean
in association with Methuen Children's Books
an imprint of Reed Consumer Books Ltd
Michelin House, 81 Fulham Road, London SW3 6RB
and Auckland, Melbourne, Singapore and Toronto

ISBN 0 603 55225 0

Printed and bound in Italy

Contents

CHAPTER ONE

The River Bank

The Mole had been working very hard all the morning, spring-cleaning his little home. First with brooms, then with dusters; then on ladders with a brush and a pail of whitewash; till he had splashes of whitewash all over his black fur, an aching back and weary arms.

Spring was moving in the air above and in the earth below and around him, penetrating even his dark and lowly little house with its spirit of divine discontent and longing. It was small wonder, then, that he suddenly flung down his brush on the floor, said "Bother!" and "Hang spring-cleaning!" and bolted out of the house.

He scraped and scratched and scrabbled and scrooged, working busily with his little paws and muttering, "Up we go! Up we go!" till at last pop! his snout came out into the sunlight, and he found himself rolling in the warm grass of a great meadow.

"This is fine!" he said to himself. "This is better than whitewashing!" and he jumped off all his four legs at once, in the joy of living and the delight of spring without its cleaning.

He thought his happiness was complete when, as he meandered aimlessly along, suddenly he stood by the edge of a full-fed river. Never in his life had he seen a river before. All was a-shake and a-shiver – glints and gleams and sparkles, rustle and swirl, chatter and bubble. The Mole was bewitched. As he sat on the grass, a dark hole in the bank opposite, just above the water's edge, caught his eye. Then, as he looked, a small face appeared. A little brown face, with whiskers.

It was the Water Rat!

"Hullo, Mole!" he said. "Would you like to come over?"

"Oh, it's all very well to *talk*," said the Mole, rather pettishly, he being new to riverside life and its ways.

The Rat said nothing, but stepped into a little boat which the Mole had not observed and sculled smartly across.

"Now then, step lively!" he said, holding up his fore-paw as the Mole stepped gingerly down, and the Mole, to his surprise and rapture, found himself seated in the stern of a real boat.

"Do you know," he said, "I've never been in a boat before in all my life."

"What?" cried the Rat, open-mouthed. "Never been in a – you never – well, I – what have you been doing then?"

"Is it so nice as all that?" asked the Mole shyly.

"Nice? It's the *only* thing," said the Water Rat solemnly. "Believe me, my friend, there is *nothing* half so much worth doing as messing about in boats. Look here! Supposing we drop down the river together, and have a long day of it?"

The Mole waggled his toes from sheer happiness. "*What* a day I'm having!" he said. "Let us start at once!"

"Hold hard a minute, then!" said the Rat and climbed up into his hole above. He reappeared with a fat, wicker luncheon-basket.

"What's inside it?" asked the Mole, wriggling with curiosity.

"There's cold chicken inside it," replied the Rat briefly; "coldtonguecoldhamcoldbeefpickledgherkinssalad frenchrollscresssandwidgespottedmeat gingerbeerlemonadesodawater–"

"O stop, stop," cried the Mole in ecstasies. "This is too much!"

"Do you really think so?" inquired the Rat. "It's only what I always take on these little excursions."

"All this is so new to me," said the Mole. "Do you really live by the river? What a jolly life!"

"By it and with it and on it and in it," said the Rat. "It's brother and sister to me, and company, and food and drink. Lord! the times we've had together.

"Now then! Here's our backwater, where we're going to lunch."

It was so very beautiful that the Mole could only hold up both fore-paws and gasp, "O my! O my! O my!"

The Rat helped the Mole safely ashore, and swung out the luncheon-basket. The Mole begged to be allowed to unpack it all by himself; and the Rat was very pleased to indulge him, and to sprawl at full length on the grass and rest.

When all was ready, the Rat said, "Now pitch in, old fellow!" and the Mole was very glad to, for he had started his spring-cleaning at a very early hour that morning, as people *will* do, and had not paused for bite or sup.

"What are you looking at?" said the Rat presently, when the edge of their hunger was somewhat dulled.

"I am looking," said the Mole, "at a streak of bubbles that I see travelling along the surface of the water."

"Bubbles? Oho!" said the Rat, in an inviting sort of way.

A broad glistening muzzle showed itself above the edge of the bank, and the Otter hauled himself out and shook the water from his coat.

"Greedy beggars!" he observed, making for the provender. "Why didn't you invite me, Ratty?"

"This was an impromptu affair," explained the Rat. "By the way – my friend Mr Mole."

"Proud, I'm sure," said the Otter, and the two animals were friends forthwith.

"Such a rumpus everywhere!" continued the Otter. "All the world seems out on the river today. Toad's out in his brand-new boat; new togs, new everything!"

The two animals looked at each other and laughed.

"Once, it was nothing but sailing," said the Rat. "Then he tired of that and took to punting. Last year it was house-boating. We all had to go and stay with him in his house-boat, and pretend we liked it. It's all the same, whatever he takes up; he gets tired of it, and starts on something fresh."

"Such a good fellow, too," remarked the Otter: "but no stability – especially in a boat!"

From where they sat they could get a glimpse of the main stream; and just then a boat flashed into view, the rower – a short, stout figure – splashing badly and rolling a good deal, but working his hardest. The Rat stood up and hailed him, but Toad – for it was he – shook his head and settled sternly to his work.

"He'll be out of the boat in a minute if he rolls like that," said the Rat, sitting down again.

"Of course he will," chuckled the Otter.

Just then, an errant May-fly swerved past. There was a swirl of water and a "cloop!" and the May-fly was visible no more.

Neither was the Otter. But again there was a streak of bubbles on the surface of the river.

"Well, well," said the Rat, "I suppose we ought to be moving. I wonder which of us had better pack the luncheon-basket?"

He did not speak as if he was frightfully eager for the treat.

"O, please let me," said the Mole. So, of course, the Rat let him.

The afternoon sun was getting low as the Rat sculled gently homewards in a dreamy mood.

The Mole was very full of lunch and already quite at home in a boat (so he thought). Presently he said, "Ratty! Please, *I* want to row, now!"

The Rat shook his head with a smile. "Not yet," he said – "wait till you've had a few lessons. It's not so easy as it looks."

The Mole was quiet for a minute or two. But he began to feel more and more jealous of Rat, sculling so easily along, and his pride began to whisper that he could do it every bit as well. He jumped up and seized the sculls, so suddenly, that the Rat was taken by surprise and fell backwards off his seat with his legs in the air.

The triumphant Mole took his place, flung his sculls back with a flourish, and made a great dig at the water. He missed the surface altogether, his legs flew up above his head and – sploosh! Over went the boat.

O my, how cold the water was, and O, how *very* wet it felt. Then a firm paw gripped him by the back of his neck. It was the Rat, and he was laughing.

He propelled the helpless Mole to shore and set him down on the bank, a squashy, pulpy lump of misery. The dismal Mole, wet without and ashamed within, trotted about till he was fairly dry, while the Rat recovered the boat and dived for the luncheon-basket.

As they set off again, the Mole said in a low voice, "Ratty, my friend! I am very sorry indeed for my foolish conduct. My heart quite fails me when I think how I might have lost that beautiful luncheon-basket. Will you forgive me?"

"That's all right, bless you!" responded the Rat cheerily. "What's a little wet to a Water Rat? Don't you think any more about it; and look here! I really think you had better come and stop with me for a little time. I'll teach you to row and to swim, and you'll soon be as handy on the water as any of us."

The Mole was so touched that he could find no voice to answer; and he had to brush away a tear or two with the back of his paw.

When they got home, the Rat made a bright fire in the parlour and planted the Mole in an arm-chair in front of it. Then he fetched down a dressing-gown and slippers for him and told him river stories till supper-time. Supper was a most cheerful meal. But shortly afterwards a terribly sleepy Mole had to be escorted upstairs by his considerate host, to the best bedroom, where he soon laid his head on his pillow in great peace and contentment.

This day was only the first of many similar ones for the Mole, each of them longer and fuller of interest as the ripening summer moved onward. He learnt to swim and to row, and entered into the joy of running water.

CHAPTER TWO

The Open Road

One bright summer morning, the Rat was sitting on the river bank, singing a little song he had just composed.

"Ratty," said the Mole suddenly, "I want to ask you a favour. Won't you take me to call on Mr Toad? I've heard so much about him, and I do so want to make his acquaintance."

"Why, certainly," said the good-natured Rat. "Get the boat out, and we'll paddle up there at once. It's never the wrong time to call on Toad. Early or late he's always glad to see you."

"He must be a very nice animal," observed the Mole, as he got into the boat.

"He is indeed the best of animals," replied Rat. "So good-natured and affectionate. Perhaps he's not very clever – we can't all be geniuses;

and it may be that he is both boastful and conceited. But he has got some great qualities, has Toady."

Rounding a bend in the river, they came in sight of a handsome old house, with well-kept lawns reaching down to the water's edge.

"There's Toad Hall," said the Rat. "Toad is rather rich, you know, and this is really one of the nicest houses in these parts, though we never admit as much to Toad."

They disembarked, and strolled across the flower-decked lawns in search of Toad, whom they found resting in a wicker garden-chair with a preoccupied expression of face, and a large map spread out on his knees.

"Hooray!" he cried, jumping up on seeing them, "this is splendid!" He shook the paws of both of them warmly, never waiting for an introduction to the Mole. "You don't know how lucky it is, your turning up just now!"

"Let's sit quiet a bit, Toady!" said the Rat, throwing himself into an easy chair, while the Mole took another by the side of him and made some civil remark about Toad's "delightful residence".

"Finest house on the whole river," cried Toad boisterously. "Or anywhere else, for that matter," he could not help adding.

Here the Rat nudged the Mole. The Toad saw him do it, and turned very red. Then Toad burst out laughing.

"All right, Ratty," he said. "It's only my way, you know. Now look here. You've got to help me. It's most important!"

"It's about your rowing, I suppose," said the Rat, with an innocent air. "You're getting on fairly well, though you splash a good bit still."

"O, pooh! boating!" interrupted the Toad, in great disgust. "I've given that up *long* ago. No, I've discovered the real thing, the only genuine occupation for a lifetime. I propose to devote the remainder of mine to it. Come with me, dear Ratty, and your friend also, and you shall see what you shall see!"

He led the way to the stable-yard and there, drawn out of the coach-house, they saw a gipsy caravan, shining with newness, painted a canary-yellow picked out with green, and red wheels.

"There you are!" cried the Toad, straddling and expanding himself. "There's real life for you. The open road, the dusty highway. Here today, up and off to somewhere else tomorrow! Travel, change, interest, excitement! The whole world before you. And mind, this is the finest cart of its sort that was ever built. Come inside and look at the arrangements. Planned 'em all myself, I did!"

It was indeed very compact and comfortable. The Mole was tremendously excited, and followed him eagerly up the steps. The Rat only snorted.

"All complete!" said the Toad triumphantly. "You see – everything you can possibly want – letter-paper, bacon, jam, cards and dominoes. You'll find," he continued, as they descended the steps again, "that nothing whatever has been forgotten, when we make our start this afternoon."

"I beg your pardon," said the Rat slowly, "but did I overhear you say something about '*we*', and '*start*', and '*this afternoon*'?"

"Now, dear good old Ratty," said the Toad imploringly, "you know you've got to come. I can't possibly manage without you. I want to show you the world!"

"I don't care," said the Rat doggedly. "I'm not coming, and that's flat. And Mole's going to do as I do, aren't you, Mole?"

"Of course I am," said the Mole loyally. "All the same, it sounds as if it might have been rather fun," he added wistfully. Poor Mole! He had fallen in love with the canary-coloured cart and all its little fitments. The Rat wavered.

"Come and have some lunch," said Toad, "and we'll talk it over."

During luncheon the Toad painted the prospects of the trip and the joys of the open life and the roadside in such glowing colours that the

Mole could hardly sit in his chair for excitement. Somehow, it soon seemed taken for granted by all three of them that the trip was a settled thing; and the Rat allowed his good-nature to override his personal objections. He could not bear to disappoint his two friends.

When they were quite ready, the now triumphant Toad led his companions to the paddock and set them to capture the old grey horse, who had been told off by Toad for the dustiest job in this dusty expedition. He frankly preferred the paddock, and took a deal of catching. At last the horse was caught and harnessed, and they set off, all talking at once.

It was a golden afternoon.

Good-natured wayfarers stopped to say nice things about their beautiful cart; and rabbits held up their fore-paws, and said, "O my! O my! O my!"

Late in the evening, tired and happy and miles from home, they drew up on a remote common, and ate their simple supper sitting on the grass by the side of the cart.

After so much open air and excitement the Toad slept very soundly, and no amount of shaking could rouse him out of bed next morning. So the Mole and Rat turned to and the hard work had all been done by the time Toad appeared on the scene, remarking what a pleasant easy life it was they were all leading now.

Their way lay across country by narrow lanes, and it was not till the afternoon that they came out on the high road. There disaster sprang out on them.

They were strolling along the high road when far behind them they heard a faint warning hum, like the drone of a distant bee. Glancing back, they saw a small cloud of dust advancing on them at incredible speed, while from out of the dust a faint "Poop-poop!" wailed.

In an instant the peaceful scene was changed, and with a blast of wind and a whirl of sound that made them jump for the nearest ditch, it was on them! The "poop-poop" rang in their ears and the magnificent motor-car possessed all earth and air for the fraction of a second, flung an enveloping cloud of dust that blinded and enwrapped them utterly, and then dwindled to a speck in the far distance.

The old grey horse, dreaming, as he plodded along, of his quiet paddock, reared and plunged and drove the cart backwards towards the deep ditch at the side of the road. There was a heart-rending crash – and the canary-coloured cart, their pride and their joy, lay on its side in the ditch, an irredeemable wreck.

The Rat danced up and down in the road. "You villains!" he shouted, shaking both fists. "You road-hogs! – I'll have the law on you!"

Toad sat down in the middle of the dusty road, his legs stretched out before him, and stared in the direction of the disappearing motor-car. His face wore a placid, satisfied expression, and at intervals he faintly murmured "Poop-poop!"

The Mole went to look at the cart, on its side in the ditch. It was indeed a sorry sight. The Rat came to help him, but their united efforts were not sufficient to right the cart. "Hi! Toad!" they cried. "Come and bear a hand, can't you!"

Toad never answered a word, or budged from his seat in the road.

"Glorious, stirring sight!" he murmured. "The *real* way to travel! O bliss! O poop-poop! O my! O my!

"And to think that I never *knew*! But *now* – what dust-clouds shall spring up behind me as I speed on my reckless way!"

"What are we to do with him?" asked the Mole.

"Nothing at all," replied the Rat firmly. "He has got a new craze, and it always takes him that way, in its first stage. Come on!" he said grimly. "It's five or six miles to the nearest town, and we shall just have to walk it. "Now, look here, Toad! You'll have to go straight to the police-station and lodge a complaint. And then arrange for the cart to be mended."

"Police-station! Complaint!" murmured Toad dreamily. "Me *complain* of that beautiful, that heavenly vision! *Mend* the *cart!* I've done with carts forever. I never want to see the cart, or to hear of it, again."

The Rat turned from him in despair. "He's quite hopeless," he said to the Mole.

On reaching the town they went straight to the railway-station. Eventually, a slow train landed them at a station not far from Toad Hall. They escorted the spell-bound, sleep-walking Toad to his door and put him to bed. Then they got out their boat and sculled down the river home.

The following evening the Mole was sitting on the bank fishing when the Rat came strolling along to find him. "Heard the news?" he said. "There's nothing else being talked about, all along the river bank. Toad went up to Town by an early train this morning. And he has ordered a large and very expensive motor-car!"

CHAPTER THREE

The Wild Wood

The Mole had long wanted to make the acquaintance of the Badger. He seemed to be such an important personage. But whenever the Mole mentioned his wish to the Water Rat he always found himself put off.

"Couldn't you ask him here – dinner or something?" said the Mole.

"He wouldn't come," replied the Rat simply. "Badger hates Society, and invitations, and all that sort of thing."

"Well, then, supposing we go and call on *him*," suggested the Mole.

"O, I'm sure he wouldn't like that at *all*," said the Rat, quite alarmed. "He's so very shy, he'd be sure to be offended. Besides, we can't. He lives in the very middle of the Wild Wood."

The Mole had to be content with this and it was not till summer was long over, and cold and frost kept them much indoors, that he found his thoughts dwelling again on the solitary grey Badger, who lived his own life by himself, in the middle of the Wild Wood.

In the winter time the Rat slept a great deal. During his short day he scribbled poetry or did small domestic jobs about the house and, of course, there were always animals dropping in for a chat.

Still the Mole had a good deal of spare time on his hands, and so one afternoon, when the Rat in his armchair was alternately dozing and trying over rhymes that wouldn't fit, he formed the resolution to go out and explore the Wild Wood, and perhaps strike up an acquaintance with Mr Badger.

It was a cold still afternoon with a hard steely sky overhead, when he slipped out of the

warm parlour into the open air. The country lay bare and entirely leafless around him. With great cheerfulness of spirit he pushed on towards the Wild Wood, which lay before him low and threatening.

There was nothing to alarm him at first. Twigs crackled under his feet, logs tripped him, funguses on stumps startled him for a moment, but that was all fun, and exciting.

Then the faces began.

He thought he saw a little evil face, looking out at him from a hole. He quickened his pace, telling himself cheerfully not to begin imagining things, or there would be simply no end to it. He passed another hole, and another; and then – yes! – no! – yes! certainly a little narrow face flashed up and was gone. He hesitated – and strode on. Then suddenly there were hundreds of them, coming and going rapidly, all hard-eyed and evil and sharp.

Then the whistling began.

Very faint and shrill it was, and far behind him, when first he heard it. Then it broke out on either side. They were up and alert and ready, whoever they were! And he was alone, and far from help and the night was closing in.

Then the pattering began.

Was it in front or behind? It seemed to be closing in on him, hunting, chasing something or – somebody? In panic, he began to run too. He ran up against things, he fell over things and into things, he darted under things and dodged round things. At last he took refuge in the deep dark hollow of an old beech tree. He was too tired to run any further and could only snuggle down into the dry leaves and hope he was safe.

Meantime the Rat, warm and comfortable, dozed by his fireside. Then a coal slipped, the fire crackled and he woke with a start. He reached down to the floor for his verses, and then looked round for the Mole to ask him if he knew a rhyme for something or other. But the Mole was not there. He called "Moly!" several times, and, receiving no answer, got up and went out into the hall. The Mole's cap and goloshes were gone.

The Rat left the house hoping to find the Mole's tracks. There they were, sure enough. He could see the imprints in the mud, leading direct to the Wild Wood. The Rat looked very grave.

Then he re-entered the house, strapped a belt round his waist, shoved a brace of pistols into it, took up a stout cudgel and set off for the Wild Wood at a smart pace.

Here and there wicked little faces popped out of holes, but vanished immediately at sight of the valorous animal, his pistols and the great ugly cudgel in his grasp. He made his way through the length of the wood, all the time calling out cheerfully, "Moly, Moly, Moly! Where are you? It's me – old Rat!"

At last to his joy he heard a feeble voice, saying, "Ratty! Is that really you?" The Rat crept into the hollow, and found the Mole exhausted and still trembling. "O Rat!" he cried, "I've been so frightened!"

"O, I quite understand," said the Rat soothingly. "You shouldn't really have gone and done it, Mole. I did my best to keep you from it."

"Surely the brave Mr Toad wouldn't mind coming here by himself, would he?" inquired the Mole.

"Old Toad?" said the Rat, laughing. "He wouldn't show his face here alone, not for a whole hatful of golden guineas."

The Mole was greatly cheered by the Rat's laughter and the sight of his stick and his gleaming pistols.

"Now, then," said the Rat, "we really must make a start for home. It will never do to spend the night here."

"Dear Ratty," said the poor Mole. "I'm dreadfully sorry, but you must let me rest here a while longer, if I'm to get home at all."

"O, all right," said the good-natured Rat, "rest away."

So the Mole got well into the dry leaves and stretched himself out, and presently dropped off into sleep.

When he woke up, the Rat went to the entrance of their retreat and put his head out. Then the Mole heard him saying quietly to himself, "Hullo! hullo! here – *is* – a – go!"

"What's up, Ratty?" asked the Mole.

"*Snow* is up," replied the Rat briefly, "or rather, *down*. It's snowing hard."

The Mole crouched beside him, and, looking out, saw a gleaming carpet springing up everywhere. A fine powder filled the air and caressed the cheek.

"Well, well, it can't be helped," said the Rat. "We must make a start. The worst of it is, this snow makes everything look so very different."

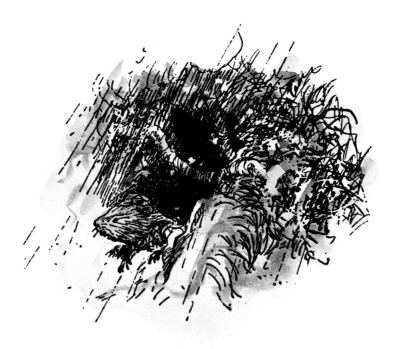

It did indeed. The Mole would not have known that it was the same wood. However, they set out bravely, and took the line that seemed most promising.

An hour or two later they pulled up, dispirited, weary, and hopelessly at sea. The snow was so deep that they could hardly drag their little legs through it. There seemed to be no way out.

"Look here," said the Rat. "There's a sort of dell down there. We'll make our way down into that, and try and find some sort of shelter."

They struggled down and hunted about for a corner that was dry. Suddenly the Mole tripped and fell forward with a squeal.

"O, my leg!" he cried. "O my poor shin!"

"Poor old Mole!" said the Rat kindly. "Let's have a look."

"I must have tripped over a branch," said the Mole miserably.

"It's a very clean cut," said the Rat. "Looks as if it was made by a sharp edge of something in metal. Funny!"

"Well, never mind what done it," said the Mole, forgetting his grammar in his pain. "It hurts just the same."

But the Rat had left him and was busy scraping in the snow. Suddenly he cried, "Hooray!" and then, "Hooray-ooray-ooray-ooray!" and fell to executing a feeble jig in the snow.

"What *have* you found, Ratty?" asked the Mole.

"Come and see!" said the delighted Rat.

The Mole hobbled up and had a good look. "A door-scraper! Well, what of it? Why dance jigs round a door-scraper?"

"But don't you see what it *means*, you – you dull-witted animal?" cried the Rat impatiently. And he set to work again and made the snow fly all around him. After some further toil, a very shabby door-mat lay exposed to view.

"There, what did I tell you?" exclaimed the Rat in triumph.

"Absolutely nothing," replied the Mole. "Can we *eat* a door-mat? Or sleep under a door-mat, you exasperating rodent?"

"Do – you – mean – to – say," cried the excited Rat, "that this door-mat doesn't *tell* you anything? Scrape and dig if you want to sleep dry and warm tonight, for it's our last chance!"

The Rat attacked a snow-bank beside them, digging with fury; and the Mole scraped busily too, to oblige the Rat. At last, the result of their labours stood full in view of the astonished Mole. In the side of what had seemed to be a snow-bank stood a solid little door. On a small brass plate, neatly engraved, they could read:

MR BADGER

The Mole fell backwards from sheer surprise. "Rat!" he cried, "you're a wonder! If I only had your head – "

"But as you haven't," interrupted the Rat rather unkindly, "get up at once and hang on to that bell-pull and ring as hard as you can, while I hammer!"

While the Rat attacked the door with his stick, the Mole sprang up at the bell-pull, clutched it and swung there, both his feet well off the ground, and from quite a long way off they could faintly hear a deep-toned bell respond.

They waited patiently for what seemed a very long time. At last they heard the sound of slow shuffling footsteps. There was the noise of a bolt shot back, and the door opened a few inches.

"Now, the *very* next time this happens," said a gruff voice, "I shall be exceedingly angry. Who is it?"

"O, Badger," cried the Rat, "It's me, Rat, and my friend Mole, and we've lost our way in the snow."

"What, Ratty, my dear little man!" exclaimed the Badger, in quite a different voice. "Come along in, both of you. Why, you must be perished."

The two animals tumbled over each other in their eagerness to get inside. The Badger looked kindly down on them and patted both their heads.

"This is not the sort of night for small animals to be out," he said. "Come along into the kitchen. There's a first-rate fire there, and supper and everything."

He shuffled on in front of them and they followed him down a long, gloomy passage, into the glow and warmth of a large fire-lit kitchen. The oaken settles exchanged cheerful glances with each other; plates on the dresser grinned at pots on the shelf, and the merry firelight flickered and played over everything. The kindly Badger thrust them down on a settle to toast themselves at the fire and bathed the Mole's shin and mended the cut with sticking-plaster till the whole thing was just as good as new, if not better.

When they were thoroughly toasted, the Badger summoned them to the table. When they saw the supper that was spread for them, really it seemed only a question of what they should attack first.

Conversation was impossible for a long time; and when it was slowly resumed, it was that regrettable sort of conversation that results from talking with your mouth full. The Badger did not mind that sort of thing at all, nor did he take any notice of elbows on the table, or everybody speaking at once. He nodded gravely as the animals told their story; and he did not seem surprised or shocked at anything, and he never said, "I told you so," or remarked that they ought to have done so-and-so. The Mole began to feel very friendly towards him.

When supper was finished at last, they gathered round the fire and the Badger said heartily, "Now then! tell us the news. How's old Toad going on?"

"O, from bad to worse," said the Rat gravely. "Another smash-up only last week. This is the seventh."

"He's been in hospital three times," put in the Mole; "and as for the fines he's had to pay, it's awful to think of!"

"Yes," continued the Rat. "Toad's rich, but he's not a millionaire. And he's a hopelessly bad driver. Badger! We're his friends – oughtn't we to do something?"

The Badger went through a bit of hard thinking. "Now look here!" he said at last. "You know I can't do anything *now*?"

His two friends assented. No animal is ever expected to do anything strenuous or heroic during the winter. "But," continued the Badger, "once the year has really turned, *then* we'll take Toad seriously in hand. We'll *make* him be a sensible Toad. You're asleep, Rat!"

"Not me!" said the Rat, waking up with a jerk.

"He's been asleep two or three times since supper," said the Mole, laughing.

"Well, it's time we were all in bed," said the Badger. "I'll show you your quarters. And take your time tomorrow – breakfast at any hour you please!"

The two tired animals came down to breakfast very late next morning, and found two young hedgehogs sitting on a bench, eating porridge.

"Where's Mr Badger?" inquired the Mole.

"The master's gone into his study, sir," replied a hedgehog. "He said as how he was going to be particular busy this morning, and on no account was he to be disturbed."

This explanation was thoroughly understood by everyone present.

The animals well knew that Badger, having eaten a hearty breakfast, had retired to his study and settled in an armchair with his legs up on another and a red cotton handkerchief over his face, and was being "busy" in the usual way at this time of the year.

The front-door bell clanged loudly and in walked the Otter.

"Thought I should find you here," he said cheerfully. "They were in a state of alarm along the River Bank this morning. Rat never been home all night – nor Mole either. But I knew that when people were in any fix they mostly went to Badger, so I came straight here, through the Wild Wood."

"Weren't you at all – er – nervous?" asked the Mole.

The Otter showed a gleaming set of strong white teeth as he laughed. "I'd give 'em nerves if any of them tried anything on with me."

Just then Badger entered, yawning and rubbing his eyes, and they all sat down to luncheon together. The Mole took the opportunity to tell Badger how home-like it all felt to him. "Once well underground," he said, "nothing can get at you."

The Badger beamed on him. "That's exactly what I say," he replied. "And then, if your ideas get larger, a dig and a scrape and there you are! If you feel your house is a bit too big, you stop up a hole or two. No builders, no tradesmen and, above all, no *weather*. When lunch is over, I'll take you round this little place of mine."

So after luncheon, Badger lighted a lantern and bade the Mole follow him. The Mole was staggered at the size of it all. "How on earth," he said, "did you find time and strength to do all this?"

"As a matter of fact I did none of it – only cleaned out the passages," said the Badger simply. "You see very long ago, there was a city of people here."

"But what has become of them all?" asked the Mole.

"Who can tell?" said the Badger. "People come and go. But we remain. Badgers are an enduring lot."

When they got back to the kitchen again, they found the Rat walking up and down, very restless. He seemed to be afraid that the river would run away if he wasn't there to look after it.

"Come along, Mole," he said anxiously. "We must get off. Don't want to spend another night in the Wild Wood."

"It'll be all right," said the Otter. "I'm coming with you, and if there's a head that needs to be punched, you can confidently rely upon me to punch it."

"You needn't fret, Ratty," added the Badger placidly. "When you have to go, you shall leave by one of my short cuts."

The Rat was nevertheless still anxious to be off, so the Badger led the way along a damp and airless tunnel for a distance that seemed to be miles. At last daylight began to show through the mouth of the passage. The Badger, bidding them good-bye, pushed them through the opening and retreated.

They found themselves standing on the very edge of the Wild Wood: rocks and brambles and tree-roots behind them; in front, quiet fields and, far ahead, a glint of the familiar old river.

CHAPTER FOUR
Mole's Christmas

Some days later, Mole and Rat were returning across country after a long day's outing with Otter. The shades of the short winter day were closing in, and they had still some distance to go.

They plodded along steadily and silently, each of them thinking his own thoughts. The Rat was walking a little way ahead, as his habit was, his eyes fixed on the straight grey road in front of him; so he did not notice poor Mole when suddenly the summons reached him, and took him like an electric shock.

It was a mysterious call that suddenly reached Mole in the darkness, making him tingle through and through with its very familiar appeal, even while as yet he could not clearly remember what it was. He stopped dead in his tracks, his nose searching hither and thither. A moment, and he had caught it again; and with it came recollection in fullest flood.

Home! That was what they meant, those caressing appeals, wafted through the air! Why, it must be quite close by him at that moment, his old home that he had hurriedly forsaken that day when he first found the river! Since his escape on that bright morning he had hardly given it a thought. Now, with a rush of old memories, how clearly it stood up before him in the darkness!

"Ratty!" he called, full of joyful excitement, "hold on! Come back!"

"*Come* along Mole!" replied the Rat cheerfully, still plodding along.

"*Please* stop, Ratty!" pleaded the poor Mole, in anguish. "You don't understand! It's my old home! I've just come across the smell of it. I *must* go to it, I must. Please, please come back!"

The Rat was far ahead, too far to hear what the Mole was calling.

"Mole, we mustn't stop now, really!" he called back. "It's late and the snow's coming on again."

Poor Mole stood in the road, his heart torn asunder. But his loyalty to his friend stood firm. With an effort he caught up the unsuspecting Rat, who began chattering cheerfully about what they would do when they got back, never noticing his companion's silence and distress. At last, however, he stopped and said kindly, "Look here, Mole old chap, you seem dead tired. We'll sit down for a minute and rest."

The Mole subsided forlornly on a tree-stump. The sob he had fought with so long refused to be beaten and he cried freely and helplessly.

The Rat, dismayed, did not dare to speak for a while. At last he said, very quietly, "What is it, old fellow? Whatever is the matter?"

Poor Mole found it difficult to get any words out.

"I know it's a – shabby, dingy little place," he sobbed at last, "but it was my own little home – and I was fond of it and I smelt it suddenly when I called and you wouldn't listen, Rat – and everything came back to me with a rush – and I *wanted* it! – O dear, O dear!"

The Rat stared straight in front of him saying nothing. After a time he muttered gloomily, "I see it all now! What a *pig* I have been! A pig – that's me!" Then he rose from his seat, and, remarking carelessly, "Well, now we'd really better be getting on, old chap!" set off up the road again, over the toil-some way they had come.

"Wherever are you (hic) going to (hic)?" cried the tearful Mole.

"We're going to find that home of yours," replied the Rat pleasantly. "You had better come along. It will take some finding, and we shall want your nose."

They moved on in silence for some little way, when suddenly Mole stood rigid, while his uplifted nose, quivering slightly, felt the air. Suddenly, without warning, Mole dived and Rat followed him down the tunnel to which his nose had faithfully led him.

Facing them was Mole's little front door, with "Mole End" painted, in Gothic lettering, over the bell-pull at the side.

Mole's face beamed. He lit a lamp, and took one glance round his old home. He saw the dust lying thick on everything, the cheerless, deserted look of the neglected house – and collapsed on a chair. "O Ratty!" he cried. "Why did I bring you to this poor, cold little place!"

The Rat paid no heed. "What a capital little house this is!" he called out cheerily. "We'll make a jolly night of it. First we want a good fire." The Rat soon had a cheerful blaze roaring, but Mole had another fit of the blues.

"Rat," he moaned, "how about supper? I've nothing to give you."

"What a fellow you are for giving in!" said the Rat reproachfully. "Come with me and forage."

They went and foraged and found a tin of sardines, a box of biscuits and a German sausage.

"There's a banquet for you!" observed the Rat.

"No bread!" groaned the Mole. "No butter, no –"

"No *pâté de foie gras*, no champagne!" continued the Rat, grinning.

He had just got to work with the sardine-opener when sounds were heard from the fore-court.

"What's up?" inquired the Rat.

"It must be the field-mice," replied the Mole. "They go round carol-singing regularly at this time of year."

"Let's have a look at them!" cried the Rat, running to the door.

In the fore-court stood some eight or ten little field-mice. They glanced shyly at each other, sniggering a little, and their little voices uprose on the air.

"Well sung, boys!" cried the Rat heartily when the voices ceased. "Now come along in and warm yourselves."

"Yes, come along," cried Mole eagerly. "Now, you just wait a minute, while we – O Ratty!" he cried in despair. "We've nothing to give them!"

"You leave all that to me," said the Rat. "Here, you with the lantern! Are there any shops open at this hour?"

"Why, certainly, sir," replied the field-mouse. Much muttered conversation ensued. Finally, there was a chink of coins, the field-mouse was provided with a basket and off he hurried. The rest of the field-mice perched in a row on the settle and toasted their chilblains.

Soon the field-mouse with the lantern reappeared, staggering under the weight of his basket. Under the generalship of Rat, everybody was set to do something or to fetch something. In a very few minutes supper was ready, and Mole saw his little friends' faces brighten and beam as they fell to without delay; and then let himself loose on the provender, thinking what a happy home-coming this had turned out, after all.

When the door had closed on the last of them, the Rat, with a tremendous yawn, said, "Mole, old chap, I'm ready to drop," and he clambered into his bunk and rolled himself up in the blankets. The weary Mole also was glad to turn in. But ere he closed his eyes he let them wander round his old room. He did not want to abandon his new life, to turn his back on sun and air. But it was good to think he had this to come back to, this place which was all his own and could always be counted upon for the same simple welcome.

CHAPTER FIVE

Toad's Adventures

It was a bright morning in the early part of summer. The Mole and the Water Rat had been up since dawn very busy on matters connected with boats and the opening of the boating season; painting and varnishing and mending paddles and so on.

They were finishing breakfast in their little parlour when a heavy knock sounded at the door.

"Bother!" said the Rat, all over egg. "See who it is, Mole, like a good chap."

The Mole went to attend the summons, and the Rat heard him utter a cry of surprise. Then he flung the parlour door open, and announced with much importance, "Mr Badger!"

This was a wonderful thing, indeed, that the Badger should pay a formal call on them, or indeed on anybody. The Badger strode into the room with an expression full of seriousness.

"The hour has come!" he said with great solemnity.

"What hour?" asked the Rat uneasily, glancing at the clock on the mantelpiece.

"Why, Toad's hour!" replied the Badger. "The hour of Toad! I said I would take him in hand as soon as the winter was well over, and I'm going to take him in hand to-day!"

"Toad's hour, of course!" cried the Mole. "I remember now! *We'll* teach him to be a sensible Toad!"

"This very morning," continued the Badger, "another new and exceptionally powerful motor-car will arrive at Toad Hall. We must be up and doing ere it is too late. You two animals will accompany me instantly to Toad Hall, and the work of rescue shall be accomplished."

"Right you are!" cried the Rat. "We'll convert him! He'll be the most converted Toad that ever was before we've done with him!"

They set off on their mission of mercy and reached Toad Hall to find a shiny new motor-car standing in front of the house. As they neared the door it was flung open, and Mr Toad, arrayed in goggles, cap and gaiters, came swaggering down the steps.

"Hullo!" he cried cheerfully. "You're just in time to come with me for a jolly – to come – for a – er – jolly – "

His hearty accents faltered as he noticed the stern look on the countenances of his silent friends.

The Badger strode up the steps. "Take him inside," he said sternly to his companions. Then, as Toad was hustled through the door, struggling and protesting, he turned to the chauffeur in charge of the new motor-car and said, "I'm afraid Mr Toad has changed his mind.

He will not require the car." Then he followed the others inside and shut the door.

"Now, then!" he said to the Toad, "first of all, take those ridiculous things off!"

"Shan't!" replied Toad, with great spirit.

"Take them off him, then, you two," ordered the Badger briefly.

They had to lay Toad out on the floor, kicking and calling all sorts of names, before they could get his motor-clothes off him.

"You knew it must come to this, sooner or later, Toad," Badger explained severely. "You're getting us animals a bad name by your furious driving and your smashes and your rows with the police. Now, I don't want to be too hard on you. I'll make one more effort to bring you to reason. Come with me and hear some facts about yourself; and we'll see whether you come out of that room the same Toad that you went in."

He took Toad by the arm, led him into a room and closed the door.

"*That's* no good!" said the Rat contemptuously. "*Talking* to Toad'll never cure him. He'll *say* anything."

After three-quarters of an hour the Badger reappeared, leading by the paw a very limp and dejected Toad. His skin hung baggily about him, his legs wobbled, and his cheeks were furrowed by the tears so plentifully called forth by the Badger's moving discourse.

"Sit down, Toad," said the Badger kindly. "My friends, I am pleased to inform you that Toad has at last seen the error of his ways and has undertaken to give up motor-cars for ever. Now, Toad, I want you solemnly to repeat, before your friends here, what you admitted to me just now. First, you are sorry for what you've done, and you see the folly of it all?"

There was a long, long pause. Toad looked desperately this way and that. At last he spoke.

"No!" he said a little sullenly, but stoutly. "I'm *not* sorry. And it wasn't folly at all! It was simply glorious!"

"What?" cried the Badger, greatly scandalized. "Didn't you tell me just now, in there –"

"O, yes, yes, in *there*," said Toad impatiently. "I'd have said anything in *there*. You're so eloquent, dear Badger, and so moving. But I'm not a bit sorry really. On the contrary, I faithfully promise that the very first motor-car I see, poop-poop! off I go in it!"

"Told you so," observed the Rat to the Mole.

"Very well," said the Badger firmly. "Since you won't yield to persuasion, we'll try what force can do. Take him upstairs, you two, and lock him up in his bedroom."

"It's for your own good, Toady," said the Rat kindly, as Toad, kicking and struggling, was hauled up the stairs by his two friends. "No more of those incidents with the police," he went on as they thrust him into his bedroom.

"No more weeks in hospital," added the Mole, turning the key.

They descended the stair, Toad shouting abuse at them through the keyhole.

"I've never seen Toad so determined," said the Badger, sighing. "However, we will see it out. He must never be left an instant unguarded."

They arranged watches accordingly, and strove to divert Toad's mind into fresh channels. But his interest in other matters did not seem to revive, and he grew apparently languid and depressed.

One morning the Rat, whose turn it was to go on duty, went upstairs to relieve Badger. "Toad's still in bed," said Badger. "Can't get much out of him. Now, you look out, Rat! When Toad's quiet and submissive, then he's at his artfullest. There's sure to be something up. Well, I must be off."

"How are you to-day, old chap?" inquired the Rat cheerfully, as he approached Toad's bedside. "Mole is going out for a run round with Badger, so I'll do my best to amuse you. Now jump up, there's a good fellow!"

"Dear, kind Rat," murmured Toad. "How little you realize my condition, and how very far I am from 'jumping up' now – if ever. But do not trouble about me. I'm a nuisance, I know."

"You are, indeed," said the Rat. "But I'd take any trouble on earth for you, if only you'd be a sensible animal."

"Then, Ratty," murmured Toad, more feebly than ever, "I beg you – for the last time, probably – to step round to the village as quickly as possible – even now it may be too late – and fetch the doctor."

"Look here, old man," said the Rat, beginning to get rather alarmed, "of course I'll fetch a doctor, if you really think you want him. But you can hardly be bad enough for that. Let's talk about something else."

"I fear, dear friend," said Toad, with a sad smile, "that 'talk' can do little in a case like this. By the way – while you are about it – would you mind asking the lawyer to step up?"

"O, he must be really bad!" the Rat said to himself as he hurried from the room, locking the door behind him. "I've known Toad fancy himself bad before, but I've never heard him ask for a lawyer! I'd better go." So he ran off on his errand of mercy.

Toad hopped lightly out of bed as soon as he heard the key turn in the lock. Then, laughing heartily, he dressed quickly and, knotting the sheets from his bed together and tying one end round the window, he slid to the ground and marched off whistling a merry tune.

It was a gloomy luncheon for Rat when Badger and Mole returned and he had to face them at table with his pitiful story.

Meanwhile, Toad was walking briskly along, some miles from home.
   "Smart piece of work that!" he remarked to himself, chuckling. "Poor old Ratty! A worthy fellow, but very little intelligence. I must take him in hand some day and see if I can make something of him."
   He strode along till he reached a little town, where the sign of "The Red Lion" reminded him that he was exceedingly hungry. He marched into the inn and sat down to eat.

He was about half-way through his meal when a familiar sound made him start and fall a-trembling all over. The poop-poop! drew nearer, the car could be heard to turn into the inn-yard, and Toad had to hold on to the leg of the table to conceal his overmastering emotion.

Presently, the party entered the room, hungry and talkative. Toad listened for a time. At last he could stand it no longer. He paid his bill and sauntered round quietly to the inn-yard. "There cannot be any harm," he said to himself, "in my only just *looking* at it!"

The car stood in the middle of the yard, quite unattended. Toad walked slowly round it, musing deeply.

"I wonder," he said to himself, "if this sort of car *starts* easily?"

Next moment, hardly knowing how it came about, he had hold of the handle and was turning it. As the familiar sound broke forth, the old passion seized on Toad and completely mastered him, body and soul. As if in a dream he found himself, somehow, seated in the driver's seat. He swung the car out through the archway, increased his pace and, as the car leapt forth on the high road, he was only conscious that he was once more Toad at his best and highest, Toad the terror, the Lord of the lone trail!

***

"This ruffian," said the Chairman of the Bench of Magistrates, "has been found guilty of stealing a valuable motor-car; of driving to the public danger, and of gross impertinence to the police. Mr Clerk, what is the very stiffest penalty we can impose for each of these offences?"

The Clerk scratched his nose. "Some people would consider," he observed, "that stealing the motor-car was the worst offence; and so it is. But cheeking the police undoubtedly carries the severest penalty; and so it ought. Supposing you were to say twelve months for the theft; three years for the furious driving, and fifteen years for the cheek, which was pretty bad sort of cheek, judging by what we've heard, those figures, added together, tot up to nineteen years. Better make it a round twenty years and be on the safe side."

"Excellent!" said the Chairman.

Then the brutal minions of the law fell upon the hapless Toad. They loaded him with chains, and dragged him from the Court House, shrieking, praying, protesting; across the market-place, below the portcullis of the grim old castle, on and on, till they reached the dungeon that lay in the innermost keep. The rusty key creaked in the lock, the great door clanged behind them; and Toad was a helpless prisoner in the remotest dungeon of the best-guarded keep of the stoutest castle in all of Merry England.

Toad flung himself on the floor, and abandoned himself to dark despair. "This is the end of everything," he said, "at least it is the end of the career of Toad, which is the same thing; the popular and handsome Toad, the Toad so free and careless and debonair! Stupid animal that I was! O wise old Badger! O intelligent Rat and sensible Mole! O unhappy and forsaken Toad!" With lamentations such as these he passed his days and nights for several weeks.

Now the gaoler had a daughter who was particularly fond of animals. This kind-hearted girl, pitying the misery of Toad, said to her father one day, "Father! I can't bear to see that poor beast so unhappy and getting so thin! Let me have the managing of him!"

Her father replied that she could do what she liked with him. He was tired of Toad and his sulks and his airs.

So that day she knocked at the door of Toad's cell.

"Cheer up, Toad," she said coaxingly. "And do try and eat a bit of dinner. I've brought you some of mine!"

But still Toad wailed and kicked with his legs, and refused to be comforted. So the wise girl retired for the time.

When she returned, some hours later, she carried a tray with a plate piled up with very hot buttered toast. The smell of that buttered toast simply talked to Toad; talked of warm kitchens, of breakfasts on frosty mornings and cosy parlour firesides on winter evenings.

Toad sat up, dried his eyes, munched his toast and soon began talking about himself and how important he was, and what a lot his friends thought of him.

The gaoler's daughter saw that the topic was doing him good and encouraged him to go on. When she said good night, Toad was very much the same self-satisfied animal that he had been of old.

They had many talks together after that and the girl grew very sorry for Toad. One morning she was very thoughtful.

"Toad," she said presently, "I have an aunt who is a washerwoman."

"There, there," said Toad affably, "never mind; *I* have several aunts who *ought* to be washerwomen."

"Do be quiet, Toad," said the girl. "You talk too much, and I'm trying to think. As I said, I have an aunt who is a washerwoman. She does the washing for all the prisoners in this castle. Now, you're very rich, and she's very poor. A few pounds wouldn't make any difference to you, and it would mean a lot to her. Now, I think if she were properly approached, she would let you have her dress and bonnet and so on, and you could escape as the official washerwoman. You're very alike – particularly about the figure."

"We're *not*," said the Toad in a huff. "I have a very elegant figure – for what I am. And you wouldn't surely have Mr Toad of Toad Hall going about the country disguised as a washerwoman?"

"Then you can stop here as a Toad," replied the girl with much spirit. "I suppose you want to go off in a coach and four!"

Toad was always ready to admit himself in the wrong. "You are a good, clever girl," he said. "Introduce me to your worthy aunt, if you will be so kind."

Next evening the girl ushered her aunt into Toad's cell. In return for his cash, Toad received a cotton print gown, an apron, a shawl and a rusty black bonnet.

Shaking with laughter, the girl proceeded to "hook-and-eye" him into the gown, and tied the strings of the bonnet under his chin. "You're the very image of her," she giggled.

With a quaking heart, Toad set forth. But he was soon agreeably surprised to find how easy everything was. The washerwoman's squat figure seemed a passport for every barred door and grim gateway. The humorous sallies to which he was subjected formed his chief danger; for Toad was an animal with a strong sense of his own dignity.

He kept his temper, however, though with difficulty.

It seemed hours before he crossed the last courtyard and dodged the outspread arms of the last warder, pleading with simulated passion for just one farewell embrace. But at last he was free!

He walked quickly towards the lights of the town, not knowing what he should do next.

As he walked along, his attention was caught by some red and green lights a little way off, and the sound of the puffing and snorting of engines. "Aha!" he thought, "this is a piece of luck! A railway-station."

He made his way to the station and went to buy his ticket. He mechanically put his fingers where his waistcoat pocket should have been. But he found – not only no money, but no pocket to hold it!

To his horror he recollected that he had left both coat and waistcoat in his cell, and with them his money, keys, watch – all that makes life worth living.

Full of despair, he wandered blindly down the platform where the train was standing and tears trickled down his nose. Very soon his escape would be discovered and he would be caught and dragged back to prison. What was to be done? As he pondered, he found himself opposite the engine, which was being oiled by its affectionate driver.

"Hullo, mother!" said the engine-driver, "what's the trouble?"

"O, sir!" said Toad, crying, "I am a poor washerwoman, and I've lost all my money, and can't pay for a ticket, and I *must* get home to-night. O dear, O dear!"

"Well, I'll tell you what I'll do," said the good engine-driver. "If you'll wash a few shirts for me when you get home and send 'em along, I'll give you a ride on my engine."

The Toad's misery turned into rapture as he eagerly scrambled up into the cab of the engine.

Of course, he had never washed a shirt in his life, and couldn't if he tried; but he thought: "When I get home and have money again, I will send the engine-driver enough to pay for quite a quantity of washing."

The guard waved his flag, and the train moved out of the station. As the speed increased, Toad began to skip up and down and shout and sing, to the great astonishment of the engine-driver, who had come across washerwomen before, but never one at all like this.

They had covered many a mile, and Toad was already considering what he would have for supper as soon as he got home, when the engine-driver, with a puzzled expression on his face, said: "It's very strange, we're the last train running in this direction to-night, yet I could be sworn that I heard another following us!"

Toad ceased his frivolous antics at once. He became grave and depressed.

Presently the driver called out, "I can see it clearly now! It is an engine on our rails, coming along at a great pace! It looks as if we were being pursued! They are gaining on us fast! And the engine is crowded with policemen, waving truncheons and all shouting 'Stop, stop, stop!' "

Then Toad fell on his knees and cried, "Save me, kind Mr Engine-driver! I am not the simple washerwoman I seem! I am the well-known and popular Mr Toad, and I have just escaped from a dungeon into which my enemies had flung me! I only borrowed a motor-car while the owners were at lunch. I didn't mean to steal it; but magistrates take such harsh views of high-spirited actions."

The engine-driver looked very grave. "I fear that you have been indeed a wicked toad," he said, "and I ought to give you up to justice. But the sight of an animal in tears always makes me feel soft-hearted. So cheer up, Toad! I'll do my best and we may beat them yet!"

They piled on more coals; the furnace roared, the sparks flew, the engine leapt and swung, but still their pursuers slowly gained. The engine-driver wiped his brow and said, "I'm afraid it's no good, Toad. You see, they have the better engine. There's only one thing left for us to do, and it's your only chance, so attend very carefully to what I tell you. A short way ahead of us is a long tunnel, and on the other side of that the line passes through a thick wood. Now, I will put on all the speed I can while we are running through the tunnel. When we are through, I will put on brakes as hard as I can, and the moment it's safe to do so you must jump and hide in the wood, before they get through the tunnel and see you. Then I will go full speed ahead again, and they can chase *me* for as long as they like. Now, be ready to jump when I tell you!"

They piled on more coals and the train shot into the tunnel. They shot out at the other end into fresh air and the peaceful moonlight, and saw the wood lying dark and helpful upon either side of the line. The driver put on brakes, and as the train slowed down to almost a walking pace he called out, "Now, jump!"

Toad jumped, rolled down a short embankment, picked himself up unhurt, scrambled into the wood and hid.

Peeping out, he saw his train get up speed again and disappear. Then out of the tunnel burst the pursuing engine, roaring and whistling, her motley crew waving their weapons and shouting, "Stop! stop! stop!" When they were past, Toad had a hearty laugh.

But he soon stopped laughing when he came to consider that it was now very late and dark and cold, and he was in an unknown wood, with no money and no chance of supper and still far from home. He dared not leave the shelter of the trees, so he struck into the wood, leaving the railway far behind him.

He found the wood strange and unfriendly. An owl, swooping noiselessly, brushed his shoulder, making him jump. A fox looked him up and down in a sarcastic sort of way, and said, "Hullo, washerwoman! Half a pair of socks short this week! Mind it doesn't occur again!" and swaggered off, sniggering. Toad looked for a stone to throw at him, but could not find one, which vexed him more than anything.

At last, cold, hungry, and tired out, he sought the shelter of a hollow tree, where he made himself as comfortable a bed as he could, and slept soundly till the morning.

CHAPTER SIX

The Further Adventures of Toad

The next morning, Toad was called early by bright sunlight streaming in on him. Sitting up, he rubbed his eyes and wondered for a moment where he was; then he remembered – he was free!

Free! He was warm from end to end as he thought of the jolly world outside, waiting eagerly for him to make his triumphal entrance, anxious to help him and to keep him company, as it always had been in days of old before misfortune fell upon him. He shook himself, combed the dry leaves out of his hair with his fingers and marched forth into the comfortable morning sun.

Toad had the world all to himself, that early summer morning. He was looking, however, for something that could tell him clearly which way he ought to go. With police scouring the country for him every minute was of importance.

Presently, round a bend in the canal, came plodding a solitary horse. From ropes attached to his collar stretched a long line. Then, with a swirl of water, the barge he was drawing slid up, its sole occupant a big stout woman, one brawny arm laid on the tiller.

"Nice morning, ma'am!" she remarked to Toad.

"I dare say it is, ma'am!" responded Toad, "to them that's not in sore trouble like what I am. My married daughter sends off to me to come to her at once; so off I comes, fearing the worst. And I've left my business to look after itself – I'm in the washing and laundering line, ma'am – and now I've lost all my money, and lost my way, and as for what may be happening to my married daughter, I don't like to think!"

"Where might your married daughter be living, ma'am?" asked the barge-woman.

"She lives close to a fine house called Toad Hall," replied Toad. "Perhaps you may have heard of it."

"Toad Hall? Why, I'm going that way myself," replied the barge-woman. "I'll give you a lift."

Toad stepped lightly on board and sat down with great satisfaction. "Toad's luck again!" thought he.

"So you're in the washing business, ma'am?" said the barge-woman politely. "Are you *very* fond of washing?"

"I love it," said Toad. "I simply dote on it. Never so happy as when I've got both arms in the wash-tub!"

"What a bit of luck, meeting you!" observed the barge-woman thoughtfully.

"Why, what do you mean?" asked Toad nervously.

"Well," replied the woman. "My husband's such a fellow for shirking his work and leaving the barge to me – how am I to get on with my washing? There's a heap of things of mine in the cabin. If you'll take one or two and put them through the wash-tub, it'll be a pleasure to you, as you rightly say, and a real help to me."

"Here, you let me steer!" said Toad, now thoroughly frightened. "I might spoil your things, or not do 'em as you like."

"Let you steer?" replied the woman, laughing. "It takes practice to steer properly. Besides, it's dull work, and I want you to be happy. No, you do the washing you are so fond of."

Toad resigned himself to his fate. "I suppose any fool can *wash!*" he thought. He selected a few garments and set to.

A long half-hour passed, and every minute saw Toad getting crosser and crosser. His back ached and he noticed with dismay that his paws were getting all crinkly. He muttered words that should never pass the lips of washerwomen or Toads; and lost the soap, for the fiftieth time. A burst of laughter made him look round. The barge-woman was laughing till the tears ran down her cheeks. "I thought you must be a humbug all along,"

she gasped. "Pretty washerwoman you are! Never washed so much as a dish-clout in your life, I'll lay!"

Toad's temper fairly boiled over. "You common, low, *fat* barge-woman!" he shouted; "Washerwoman indeed! I would have you know that I am a very well known, respected, distinguished Toad!"

The woman peered under his bonnet. "Why, so you are!" she cried. "A nasty, crawly Toad in my nice clean barge! Now that is a thing I will *not* have."

One big mottled arm shot out and caught Toad by a fore-leg, while the other gripped him by a hind-leg. Then the world turned upside down and Toad found himself flying through the air. He reached the water with a loud splash, rose to the surface spluttering, and saw the barge-woman laughing; and he vowed, as he coughed and choked, to be even with her.

He struck out for the shore and started to run after the barge. Running swiftly on he overtook the horse, unfastened the tow-rope, jumped lightly on the horse's back, and urged it to a gallop. Looking back, he saw that the barge had run aground and the barge-woman was

shouting, "Stop, stop!" "I've heard that song before," said Toad, laughing, as he spurred his steed onward.

He had travelled some miles when he found he was on a wide common. Near him stood a gipsy caravan and beside it a man was sitting on a bucket turned upside down, staring into the wide world. Near by, over a fire, hung an iron pot and out of that pot came forth rich and varied smells. Toad now knew that he had not been really hungry before. This was the real thing at last and no mistake. He looked the gipsy over, and the gipsy looked at him.

Presently the gipsy remarked, "Want to sell that there horse of yours?"

Toad was completely taken aback. It had not occurred to him to turn the horse into cash, but he badly wanted ready money and a solid breakfast.

"What?" he said, "me sell this beautiful young horse of mine? O no; it's out of the question. This horse is a cut above you altogether. No, it's not to be thought of for a moment. All the same, how much might you be disposed to offer me for this beautiful young horse of mine?"

The gipsy looked the horse over. "Shillin' a leg," he said briefly.

"A shilling a leg?" cried Toad. "O no; I could not think of accepting four shillings for this beautiful young horse."

"Well," said the gipsy, "I'll make it five shillings, and that's my last word."

Toad pondered. At last he said, "Look here! You hand me over six shillings and sixpence, and as much breakfast as I can possibly eat out of that iron pot of yours. In return, I will make over to you my spirited young horse, with all the beautiful harness thrown in."

The gipsy grumbled frightfully, but he counted out six shillings and sixpence. Then he tilted the pot, and a glorious stream of hot stew gurgled into a plate. Toad stuffed, and stuffed, and stuffed. He thought that he had never eaten so good a breakfast in all his life.

When Toad had taken as much stew as he could possibly hold, he set forth again in the best possible spirits. As he tramped along, he thought of his adventures, and his pride began to swell within him. "Ho, ho!"

he said to himself, "what a clever Toad I am! There is surely no animal equal to me for cleverness in the whole world!"

He got so puffed up with conceit that he made up a song as he walked in praise of himself, and sang it at the top of his voice.

"The world has held great Heroes,
    As history-books have showed;
But never a name to go down to fame
    Compared with that of Toad!

"The Queen and her Ladies-in-waiting
    Sat at the window and sewed.
She cried, 'Look! who's that *handsome* man?'
    They answered, 'Mr Toad'."

But his pride was shortly to have a severe fall.

After some miles he reached the high road and, as he glanced along its white length, he saw approaching him a speck that turned into a dot and then into a blob, and then into something very familiar; a double note of warning, only too well known, fell on his delighted ear.

"This is something like!" said the excited Toad. "I will hail my brothers of the wheel and they will give me a lift. With luck, it may even end in my driving up to Toad Hall in a motor-car! That will be one in the eye for Badger!"

He stepped out confidently into the road to hail the motor-car; when suddenly he became very pale, his knees shook and he collapsed. The approaching car was the very one he had stolen that fatal day when all his troubles began!

He sank down in a shabby, miserable heap in the road, murmuring, "It's all over now! Prison again! O, hapless Toad!"

The terrible motor-car drew slowly nearer till at last he heard it stop just short of him. Two gentlemen got out and one of them said, "O dear! Here is a poor washerwoman who has fainted in the road! Let us take her to the village, where doubtless she has friends."

They tenderly lifted Toad into the car and proceeded on their way. When Toad heard them talk in so kind a manner, and knew that he was not recognized, his courage began to revive.

"Look!" said one of the gentlemen. "The fresh air is doing her good. How do you feel now, ma'am?"

"A great deal better, thank you, sir," said Toad in a feeble voice. "I was only thinking, if I might sit on the front seat, where I could get the fresh air full in my face, I should soon be all right again."

"What a sensible woman!" said the gentleman. "Of course you shall."

Toad was almost himself again by now. He looked about him and the old cravings rose up and took possession of him entirely. He turned to the driver at his side.

"Please, sir," he said, "would you let me try and drive for a little. It looks so easy and I should like to be able to tell my friends I had once driven a motor-car!"

The driver laughed and the gentleman said, "Bravo, ma'am! I like your spirit. Let her have a try."

Toad eagerly took the wheel, listened with affected humility to the instructions given him, and set the car in motion.

The gentlemen clapped their hands, saying, "Fancy a washerwoman driving as well as that, the first time!"

Toad went a little faster; then faster still, and faster.

He heard the gentlemen call out, "Be careful, washerwoman!" And this annoyed him and he began to lose his head.

"Washerwoman, indeed!" he shouted recklessly. "I am the Toad, the motor-car snatcher, the prison-breaker, the Toad who always escapes!"

With a cry of horror they rose and flung themselves on him. "Seize him!" they cried. "Bind him, chain him!"

Alas! they should have thought to stop the motor-car first. With a half-turn of the wheel Toad sent the car crashing through a low hedge and into the thick mud of a horse-pond.

Toad landed with a thump, picked himself up and set off, running till he was breathless and had to settle down into a walk. When he had recovered somewhat, he began to giggle.

"Ho! ho!" he cried. "Toad again! Toad, as usual, comes out on top! Clever Toad! O, how clever I am! How very clev–"

A noise behind him made him turn his head and look. O misery! O despair! About two fields off, a chauffeur and two policemen were running towards him as hard as they could go! Poor Toad pelted away again. He ran desperately, but they still gained steadily.

He struggled on blindly and wildly, when suddenly the earth failed under his feet, and splash! he found himself head over ears in deep, rapid water. In his panic he had run straight into the river!

He tried to grasp the reeds that grew along the water's edge, but the stream was so strong that it tore them out of his hands. Presently he saw that he was approaching a big dark hole in the bank, just above his head, and as the stream bore him past he caught hold of the edge and held on. As he sighed and stared before him into the hole, something twinkled in its depths – a familiar face.

It was the Water Rat!

CHAPTER SEVEN

The Return of the Hero

The Rat put out a paw, gripped Toad by the scruff of the neck and gave a great pull. The water-logged Toad came up slowly but surely. At last he stood in the hall, streaked with mud and weed, but happy and high-spirited as of old.

"O, Ratty!" he cried. "I've been through such times since I saw you last! Such trials and sufferings, all so nobly borne! Such escapes, such disguises. O, I *am* a smart Toad, and no mistake!"

"Toad," said the Water Rat, firmly, "go upstairs at once, take off that old cotton rag and clean yourself, put on some of my clothes and try and come down looking like a gentleman if you *can*; for a more shabby, bedraggled object than you are I never set eyes on! Now, stop swaggering and arguing, and be off!"

By the time Toad came down again luncheon was on the table. While they ate, Toad told the Rat all his adventures, dwelling chiefly on his own cleverness and cunning. But the more he talked and boasted, the more grave and silent the Rat became.

At last the Rat said, "Toady, don't you see what an awful ass you've been making of yourself? On your own admission you have been imprisoned, chased, insulted, jeered at and flung in the water! All because you must go and steal a motor-car. When are you going to be sensible and try and be a credit to your friends?"

Toad heaved a deep sigh and said very nicely and humbly, "Quite right, Ratty! I've been a conceited old ass, but now I'm going to be a good Toad, and not do it any more. We'll have our coffee, and then I'm going to stroll down to Toad Hall. I've had enough adventures."

"Stroll down to Toad Hall?" cried the Rat. "Do you mean to say you haven't heard about the Stoats and Weasels?"

"The Wild Wooders?" cried Toad, trembling in every limb. "What have they been doing?"

"– And how they've been and taken Toad Hall?" continued the Rat.

Toad leaned his chin on his paws; and a tear welled up in each of his eyes, and splashed on the table, plop! plop!

"Go on, Ratty," he murmured; "tell me all."

"When you got into trouble," said the Rat, "it was a good deal talked about. The Riverbankers stuck up for you, but the Wild Wood animals got very cocky, and went about saying you would never come back again! But Mole and Badger stuck out, through thick and thin that you would come back again somehow. They arranged to move into Toad Hall, and have it all ready for you when you turned up. They didn't guess what was going to happen, of course.

"One dark night a band of weasels, armed to the teeth, crept up to the front entrance; a body of desperate ferrets possessed themselves of the back-yard, and a company of skirmishing stoats occupied the conservatory.

"Mole and Badger were sitting by the fire, suspecting nothing, when those villains rushed in from every side. They beat them with sticks and turned them out into the cold and wet! And the Wild Wooders have been living in Toad Hall ever since, and going on simply anyhow! Eating your grub, drinking your drink, singing vulgar songs – and telling everybody that they've come to stay for good."

"O, have they!" said Toad, seizing a stick. "I'll soon see about that!"
"It's no good, Toad!" called the Rat. "You'll only get into trouble."
But there was no holding him. He marched down the road, his stick
over his shoulder, till he got near his front gate. Suddenly there popped
up a long yellow ferret with a gun.

"Who comes there?" said the ferret sharply.

"Stuff and nonsense!" said Toad very angrily.

The ferret brought his gun up to his shoulder. Toad dropped flat in the road, and *Bang!* a bullet whistled over his head. As Toad scampered off down the road he heard the ferret laughing.

"What did I tell you?" said the Rat. "They are all armed. You must just wait."

Still, Toad was not inclined to give in at once. So he got out the boat, and set off up the river to where the garden of Toad Hall came down to the waterside. All seemed very peaceful and deserted. Very warily he paddled up to the mouth of the creek, and was just passing under the bridge, when ... *Crash!* A great stone smashed through the bottom of the boat. It filled and sank, and Toad found himself struggling in deep water. Looking up, he saw two stoats leaning over the bridge, watching him with glee. The indignant Toad swam to shore, while the stoats laughed and laughed. Toad retraced his weary way on foot.

"Well, *what* did I tell you?" said the Rat crossly. "And look! You've lost my boat and ruined that nice suit that I lent you! Now sit down and have your supper, and be patient. We can do nothing until we have seen the Mole and the Badger, and heard their latest news. Those poor animals have been camping out, keeping a constant eye on the stoats and weasels, and planning how to get your property back for you. You don't deserve to have such loyal friends, Toad, you don't really."

They had just finished their meal when there came a knock at the door and in walked Mr Badger, looking very rough and tousled and the Mole, very shabby and unwashed.

"Hooray! Here's old Toad!" cried the Mole. "Why, you must have managed to escape, you clever Toad!"

"Don't egg him on, Mole!" said the Rat; "you know what he is like; but please tell us what the position is and what's best to be done."

"The position's about as bad as it can be," replied the Mole grumpily.

"It's quite useless to think of attacking the place," said the Badger. "They're too strong for us."

"Then it's all over," sobbed the Toad. "I shall never see my dear Toad Hall any more!"

"Cheer up, Toady!" said the Badger. "I'm going to tell you a secret."

Toad dried his eyes. Secrets had an immense attraction for him, because he never could keep one.

"There – is – an – underground – passage," said the Badger impressively, "that leads from the river bank right up into Toad Hall."

"O, nonsense! Badger," said Toad, rather airily. "I know every inch of Toad Hall. Nothing of the sort, I do assure you!"

"My young friend," said the Badger with great severity, "your father, who was a worthy animal, discovered that passage and he showed it to me. 'Don't let my son know about it,' he said. 'He's a good boy, but simply cannot hold his tongue. If he's ever in a real fix, you may tell him about it; but not before.' Now, there's going to be a big banquet tomorrow and all the weasels will be in the dining-hall, eating and drinking and suspecting nothing. No guns, no swords, no arms whatever! They will trust entirely to their excellent sentinels. Now, that tunnel leads right up under the pantry, next to the dining-hall!"

"We shall creep out into the pantry," cried the Mole.

"and rush in upon them," said the Badger.

"– and whack 'em, and whack 'em, and whack 'em!" cried the Toad.

"Very well," said the Badger, "our plan is settled. We will make all the necessary arrangements to-morrow morning."

When Toad got down next morning he found Badger reading the paper and Rat running round the room, distributing weapons in four little heaps on the floor.

Presently the Mole came tumbling in, very pleased with himself. "I've been getting a rise out of the stoats!" he said. "I put on Toad's old washerwoman dress, and off I went to Toad Hall. The sentries were on the look-out, of course, with their guns. The sergeant in charge said, 'Run away, my good woman!' 'Run away?' says I; 'it won't be me that'll be running away, in a short time from now! A hundred bloodthirsty Badgers are going to attack Toad Hall this very night,' said I. 'Six boat-loads of Rats will come up the river, while a picked body of Toads will storm the orchard. There won't be much left of you unless you clear out while you have the chance.' They were all as flustered as could be, saying, 'That's *just* like the weasels. They have fun while we are cut to pieces by bloodthirsty Badgers.' "

"O, *Moly*, how could you?" said the Rat.

"You've spoilt everything!" cried Toad.

"Mole," said the Badger, "I see you have more sense in your little finger than some have in the whole of their fat bodies. Good Mole! Clever Mole!"

Toad was simply wild with jealousy, especially as he couldn't make out for the life of him what Mole had done that was so clever.

***

When it began to grow dark, the Rat proceeded to dress them up for the expedition. There was a belt for each animal, then a sword, a cutlass, a pair of pistols, a truncheon, several sets of handcuffs, bandages and sticking-plaster, and a flask and a sandwich-case.

The Badger laughed and said, "All right, Ratty! But I'm going to do all I've got to do with this here stick."

But the Rat only said, "*Please,* Badger! I shouldn't like you to say I had forgotten *anything!*"

Badger led them along the river for a little way, then suddenly swung himself over the edge into a hole in the river bank: they were in the secret passage! It was cold, and dark, and damp, and low, and narrow. They shuffled along, till at last they heard, apparently over their heads, people shouting and cheering and stamping on the floor.

"*What* a time they're having!" said the Badger. "Come on!" They hurried along the passage till they found themselves under a trap-door. They heaved it back, and found themselves standing in the pantry, with only a door between them and their enemies.

The noise was deafening. A voice could be made out saying, "I should like to say one word about our kind host, Mr Toad." (great laughter) – "*Good* Toad, *modest* Toad!" (shrieks of merriment).

"Just let me get at him!" muttered Toad, grinding his teeth.

"– Let me sing you a little song," went on the voice, "which I have composed on the subject of Toad!"

The Badger drew himself up, took a firm grip of his stick, and cried, "The hour is come! Follow me!" And flung the door wide open.

My!

What a squealing and a squeaking and a screeching filled the air!

The mighty Badger, his whiskers bristling; Mole, black and grim; Rat, desperate and determined; Toad, frenzied with excitement, emitting Toad-whoops that chilled them to the marrow! They were but four in all, but to the panic-stricken weasels the hall seemed full of monstrous animals, whooping and flourishing enormous cudgels; and they fled with squeals of terror, through the windows, up the chimney, anywhere to get out of reach of those terrible sticks.

Up and down the hall strode the four Friends, whacking with their sticks at every head that showed itself; and in five minutes the room

was cleared. The Badger, resting from his labours, leant on his stick and wiped his honest brow.

"Mole," he said, "you're the best of fellows! Just cut along outside and see what those stoat-sentries of yours are doing. I've an idea that, thanks to you, we shan't have much trouble from *them* to-night!"

The Mole vanished promptly through a window; and the Badger bade the other two see if they could find materials for a supper. "I want some grub," he said, in that rather common way he had of speaking.

They were just about to sit down when the Mole clambered through the window, chuckling, with an armful of rifles.

"It's all over," he reported. "As soon as the stoats, who were very jumpy already, heard the uproar inside the hall, they threw down their rifles and fled. So *that's* all right!"

"Excellent and deserving animal!" said the Badger.

So they finished their supper in great joy and contentment, and presently retired to rest, safe in Toad's ancestral home, won back by matchless valour and a proper handling of sticks.

The following morning the Badger remarked: "I'm sorry, Toad, but there's a heavy morning's work in front of you. You see, we really ought to have a Banquet to celebrate this affair. It's expected of you. Invitations have to be written, and you've got to write 'em."

"What!" cried Toad, dismayed. "Me stop indoors and write a lot of rotten letters on a jolly morning like this! Certainly not! I'll be – Stop a minute, though! Why, of course, dear Badger! It shall be done."

Toad hurried to the writing-table. A fine idea had occurred to him. He *would* write the invitations; and he would give a programme of entertainment for the evening with speeches and songs by Toad! The idea pleased him mightily and he worked very hard and got all the letters finished by noon. A small weasel hurried off to deliver them.

But when the other animals came back to luncheon, the Rat caught Toad by the arm. "Now, look here, Toad!" he said. "It's about this banquet. I am very sorry, but we want you to understand that there are going to be no speeches and no songs."

Toad saw that he was trapped. They understood him, they saw through him. His pleasant dream was shattered.

"Mayn't I sing them just one *little* song?" he pleaded piteously.

"No, not *one*," replied the Rat firmly, though his heart bled as he noticed the trembling lip of the poor disappointed Toad. "It's for your own good, Toady; you know your songs and speeches are all boasting and vanity; you *must* turn over a new leaf sooner or later."

Toad remained a long while plunged in thought. At last he raised his head. "You have conquered, my friends," he said in broken accents. "It was a small thing that I asked. However, you are right. Henceforth I will be a very different Toad. But, O dear, this is a hard world!"

He left the room with faltering steps.

"I feel like a brute," said the Rat.

"I know," said the Badger gloomily. "But would you have him jeered at by stoats and weasels?"

"Of course not," said the Rat. "And, talking of weasels, it's lucky we came upon that little weasel and confiscated Toad's invitations. I had a look at one or two; they were simply disgraceful. Mole is filling up plain, simple invitation cards."

At last the hour for the banquet drew near and Toad was still sitting there, melancholy and thoughtful. His brow resting on his paw, he pondered long and deeply. Gradually he began to smile. Then he took to giggling. At last he got up, locked the door, drew the curtains, arranged all the chairs in a semicircle, and took up his position in front of them, swelling visibly. Then he bowed, coughed twice and sang to the enraptured audience that his imagination so clearly saw.

TOAD'S LAST LITTLE SONG!

The Toad – came – home!
There was panic in the parlour and howling in the hall,
There was crying in the cow-shed and shrieking in the stall,
When the Toad – came – home!

When the Toad – came – home!
There was smashing in of window and crashing in of door,
There was chivying of weasels that fainted on the floor,
When the Toad – came – home!

Bang! go the drums!
The trumpeters are tooting and the soldiers are saluting,
And the cannon they are shooting and the motor-cars are hooting,
As the – Hero – comes!

Shout – Hooray!
And let each one of the crowd try and shout it very loud,
In honour of an animal of whom you're justly proud,
For it's Toad's – great – day!

He sang this very loud, with great unction and expression; and when he had done he sang it all over again. Then he heaved a deep sigh, and went quietly down to his guests.

The animals cheered when he entered, and crowded round to say nice things about his courage and his fighting; but Toad only smiled faintly and murmured, "Not at all!" or, "On the contrary! Badger's was the master-mind; the Mole and the Water Rat bore the brunt of the fighting; I merely served in the ranks and did little or nothing." The animals were puzzled by this unexpected attitude of his; and Toad felt, as he made his modest responses, that he was an object of absorbing interest to everyone. At intervals he stole a glance at the Badger and the Rat, staring at each other with their mouths open; and this gave him the greater satisfaction. When, later, there were cries of "Toad! Speech! Song!" Toad only shook his head and raised a paw in mild protest.

He was indeed an altered Toad!

After this climax, the four animals continued to lead their lives in great contentment. Sometimes in the course of long summer evenings the friends would stroll together in the Wild Wood, now tamed, and it was pleasing to see how respectfully they were greeted by the inhabitants, and how the mother-weasels would say to their young ones, "Look, baby! There goes the great Mr Toad! And that's the gallant Water Rat, with the famous Mr Mole." But when their infants were fractious, they would quiet them by telling how, if they didn't hush, the terrible grey Badger would up and get them. This was a base libel on Badger, who was rather fond of children; but it never failed to have its full effect.